John Cave Winscombe

Tsoé, and other poems

John Cave Winscombe

Tsoé, and other poems

ISBN/EAN: 9783744723053

Printed in Europe, USA, Canada, Australia, Japan

Cover: Foto ©Andreas Hilbeck / pixelio.de

More available books at **www.hansebooks.com**

TSOÉ

AND OTHER POEMS

BY

CAVE WINSCOM

LONDON
BASIL MONTAGU PICKERING,
196, PICCADILLY
1871.

CONTENTS.

TSOÉ:

THE TALE OF A CIRCASSIAN MAIDEN.

T S O É.

IN the fertile land of the Moslem,
  Where damask roses bloom,
Where many a scarlet poppy
  Grows dusk in twilight's gloom;
In a room in a great Harëm,
  Where through the latticed wall
The day had twined a sunny beam,
  And parting let it fall;
Upon a couch with roses decked,
  And hung.with curtains gay,
Beneath a silken coverlet,
  A beauteous virgin lay.
Sleep weighed her snowy eyelids down;
  A smile was on her brow,
As though she dreamed of her native land,
  So widely distant now,
Of her gentle mother's tender care,
  Her baby sister's play,·
And of Circassia's shady bowers,
  Where first she saw the day;—
And a tear broke from her oval eye,
  And fell upon her breast,

And, like a stray pearl from the braid,
   Rolled till it found its rest
On that swelling bosom, heaved by the breath,
Ceaseless in life, and silent in death.

Sleep on, bright image of dreaming rest !
With the smile on thy brow and the tear on thy breast;
For there is not a rosebud perfectly fair,
Till the dewdrop is resting and glittering there.

Sad is the tale of the sleeping maid,
Stolen away from the giant shade
Of the mighty mountains that tower and glow
In the pure, still light of eternal snow,
Whilst the crystal streams flow clear from their base,
Bordered by flowers of exquisite grace ;
A garden below and a fortress above,
Formed by one Maker for safety and love.

It had chanced one time, at the day's repose,
That the sun went down in amber and rose,
And when the latest beam was set,
The mountains shone in glory yet,
Though of brighter hues for a while bereft,
They blushed with the roses the day had left.
And Tsoé thought, as she gazed on the glory
Of the snow-capped mountain in evening rest,
Of the sweet and wonderful ancient story
Her mother had told of the land of the bless'd,
   Where crystal fountains ever flow,
   And brilliant gems for ever glow.

She gazed on the mountain, and thought, "It is there
That this wonderful land of bliss must lie,
For surely there is nothing half so fair
As the Caucasus' snow-white purity."

Her wandering fancy led her feet
To climb the rugged mountain's side;
Scarcely the earth they seemed to meet,
So lightly did they onward glide.

Short is eve in that sunny land,
Twilight is but a sombre link
That borders on night's darker brink
Whilst day still holds it with her hand.

Thus Tsoé, wandering far and high,
Her mind in a dreamy repose
That paints each fancy with the rose,
Thought not of night that gathered nigh,
Nor of the many beasts that roam
From sunless caves in their desert home,
Till the pale moon sent a silver streak
O'er the paler mountain's snow-clad crest,
And the eagle's loud and piercing shriek
Thrilled terror in her gentle breast.
She turned, and saw, far, far in the glade,
Her hamlet buried in evening shade,
And shuddered as the chilling cloud
Wound slowly round her like a shroud;
First, all about her misty grew,—
Then, all but mist was hid from view.

There is a' wild, strange terror when we stand
With walls of rolling cloud on either hand,
Bewildering swiftness in their nearing gloom,
That forms for man a boundless, living tomb ;—
Binds not, but yet controls the power to start,
And steals through every vital to the heart.
Thus Tsoé stands, lost in a wild dismay,—
Afraid to stir, yet more afraid to stay ;
No star to guide her wandering footsteps home,
Nor teach the rover whither she may roam.
She turns towards each transient gleam of light,
Until she flieth only from the night ;
Then fear forbids the limbs to play their part,
And faintness spreads through all the beating heart.

She sinks upon a moss-clad stone ;
The rising wind makes a dismal moan,
And dry, sere leaves from the wood below
In wheeling circles upward go,
And rustle with a dismal sound,
Tumbling along the stony ground ;
Whilst to the southward, far away,
She hears the yelping jackal bay.

Then hope was fled, and the dewy air
Clung coldly round her everywhere,
Till her eyelash shone like the crystal nets
That spiders spin o'er violets.

TSOÉ.

And Tsoé cried, " Oh, where—oh, where,
The golden fields of light and air ?
I thought to find the dazzling throne
That Allah only calls his own,
Where warriors stand in glory dressed
With Houris evermore to rest ;
Where diamonds shine midst fadeless flowers
In the balmy breath of Eden's bowers,
Whilst every form you see is fair,
And peace pervades the hallowed air ;
Where fountains sparkle 'mid vases of gold,
And exquisite creepers around them enfold ;
Where lovely Peris, in garments of snow,
Backwards and forwards like meteors go.
But Eden's bowers are not for me ;
I know not whither now to flee ;
My hopes are passed in mist away,
And night usurps the place of day."
She lays her hand upon her heart ;
Alas ! its pulse is slow and chill,
As though it wearies of its part
As wearies oft the mountain rill,
Which slackens surely every hour,
Unwatered by the expected shower.

Then a footstep breaks upon her ear,
And there rings a voice both sweet and clear,
Musically soft as the strains that fall
From Roman bells at Carnival.

And a hunter's form strides out through the fog,—
Behind him there follows his faithful dog ;
And there hangs by his side a sabre gilt
With a strange device from the point to the hilt.
   His locks are unconfined and free,
   As maidens' locks are wont to be : .
   No turban binds his flowing hair,
The breath of the mountain is gambolling there,
   Wantonly waving to and fro
   Till it tangles with the scarf below.
   His eye is of that mingled hue,
   A mellow grey or sombre blue;
   And in its clear and restless fire
   Resolve seems blent with truth and ire.
   Blue is the mantle round his form,
   Though faded by the sun and storm,
   And from that mantle's inmost fold
   There shines a cross of purest gold.
   He started when he saw the maid
   Reclining 'neath the pine-tree shade,
   And in a voice surprised, but clear,
   He asked her, "Wherefore wander here ?
   Dost thou not know the wolf and bear
   At night steal from their secret lair ?
   And that from yonder piles of snow
   The avalanche is hurled below ? "
   He took her gently by the hand
   And led her to the lower land,
   Where, like a globe of silvery light,
   Fair Cynthia rode upon the night.

And many stars like lanterns gloam
Suspended to the azure dome.
Here first they pause, to gaze for a space
On views of excelling beauty and grace ;
Then Tsoé told him all her story ;—
How she looked on the mountains in evening glory,
And thought that Allah must be there,
And all the hosts of Houris fair,
Where flowers never fade nor die,
And kindness speaks from every eye.

The warrior listened with a smile,
And held her hand in his the while,
And when she ceased he gently showed
That Eden lies beyond the flood,
And o'er its bright dominions fair
The Crucified is Ruler there.
Long did they commune, till the day
Spread o'er the east his foremost ray,
But ere they parted gave their plight
To meet again the coming night.

Fair Love ! how magic is thy power !
Queen of a life ! child of an hour !
Sometimes like a meteor darting,
Ere we meet we think of parting,
And sometimes long, and sure, and slow,
Deepening as we onward go ;
Ever bringing joy and sorrow ;
Ever hoping for to-morrow ;

Like the river ever blending
Where the ocean waves are bending,
Or like spring-time dying away,
Lost in the glowing summer day..
And so, 'twixt meeting hearts and eyes,
Bright, airy, wingéd Cupid flies,
Until a mutual feeling glows,
And then the tender passion flows,
In union knitting heart with heart,
Until it seems they ne'er can part.

O'er Tsoé thus Love's magic power
Had cast its light though binding chain,
And oft she thought upon the hour
When she should see her friend again.
So swift does Love's alluring art
Make captive of the southern heart.
She did know from whence he came,
His birth, his lineage, his name,
And yet her hand, her heart, her all,
She would have yielded to his call.
But ere the night could form a screen
For her to steal away unseen,
Her freedom was for ever gone,
And she was an imprisoned one.

For Tsoé, a slave by the harsh law of birth,
That values a woman at half of her worth,
Gives power to parents of pitiless mould
To barter their children for riches and gold.

She was sold by her father, a covetous chief,—
The small gain she brought him his only grief;
  For when the trader came to buy,
  Tsoé, with plaintive, wailing cry,
  Wept through the long and sultry day,
  Till half her beauty passed away;
  And when at eve her father brought
  The scowling Turk to see his prize,
  A passing stranger would have thought
  There was no lustre in those eyes;
For clouded and cold was the violet hue,
And under each eyelid a broad band of blue,
Swollen and reddened by many a tear,
The silent result of horror and fear;
And the smiling play of those lips was gone,
And the rose of the cheek was pale and wan,
And there was not a look nor a gesture there
But was stamped with the dye of unshaded despair.
"Chief," said the Turk, " is this the fair flower
You boasted would grace the Pasha's bower?
This pale, blighted lily is scarcely worth
The pain that she cost her mother in birth;
But since our bargain is partly proclaimed,
I'll give you the half of the sum you have named;
For though this poor flower is withered and cold,
I can see that the stem is of exquisite mould."

The night was cold, and drear, and chill,
Swoln the flood of each mountain rill;

The moon looked out from a bank ot cloud
Pale as a corse 'neath pall and shroud;
The pitiless blast made a dismal moan
O'er oak in the forest or crumbling stone,
And there remained but one small star in view,
Set in a lake of ethereal blue ;
Whilst all around was dark, dismal, and drear,
Like a desert that skirts a haunted mere.
And sometimes you heard the distant roaring
Of ceaseless cataracts onward pouring ;
And the wolves' harsh cry broke loud and shrill
As in leaguering packs they scoured the hill.

By Terek's wave gleams many a spear,
And slaves, upon their shoulders, lean
A closely curtained palanquin,
Painted with colours gay and clear.
There Tsoé sits, cold, silent, and alone,
Not a word, nor a tear, nor sigh, nor groan,
Could break from her lip, nor stream from her eye,
For strong feeling seemed numbed with agony,
As one wild passion held sway o'er her heart,
And sharpened the edge of base slavery's dart.
The trader rode at the head of the host,
Silent and calm to the outward eye,
As some old spectral midnight ghost,
That breathed in years long since gone by;—
But in that calm and rigid form
Slept many a passion's hidden storm.

TSOÉ.

Well skilled was he in arts of war,
And fiercely fell his scimitar ;
But he was lord of baser strife :
Men said that the assassin's knife
Had stained his hand with treachery's dye,
That there must rest eternally.
But none dare thwart him ; all must cower
Before his vast but cruel power,
For in the Pasha's name he sought
New beauties, whom with gold he bought,
To grace the Harem's sunny bowers,
Fresh buds amongst its withering flowers.

They wander on from day to day
By many a verdant scene and way,
Or traverse many a woody dell
Where crystal fountains fling their spray,
And where the gentle young gazelle
Sports through the long and sunny day ;
Past gurgling streams, and woody glade,
By mountain, rock, and forest shade ;
Past crumbling stones, tradition's page,
Wrapt in the mystery of age,
Where subtle snakes in secret crawl,
And lizards glitter on the wall,—
Till a lordly city rose to view
With orange groves, and vineyards fair,
And flowers of every varied hue
That fill with fragrance all the air ;

And from the stately groves arise,
In massive grandeur to the skies,
Great mosques and obelisks, that glow
And glitter in the noonday light,
With costly marble, pure as snow,
Or alabaster crystal white,
And golden minarets that shine
In brilliant splendour round their shrine.
And many streams of water clear
Go winding through the fertile plain,
Which spread their freshness everywhere
And circle many an ancient fane,
Glittering in the evening breeze
Like silvery threads amongst the trees.

Such views as these met Tsoé's eyes—
Those eyes that were of yore so bright ;
She gazed with pensive, sad surprise
Upon the scene of matchless light.
Her cheek had lost its rosy dye ;
Her thoughts seemed wrapt in settled gloom ;
She looked like that cold imagery
Which sculptors place above the tomb,—
Stonily beautiful, deathlike, but fair,

Clad in the pale robes of icy despair.
Leave her in silence, leave her in sadness ;
Words cannot comfort, and tears cannot aid ;
Smiles will not wake one faint ray of gladness ;
Leave her alone in her palanquin shade.

Follow her not to the dark gilded Harem;
Leave her to fade and to wither alone,
Beautifully pale as blows the fair arum,
Silent and cold, without even a moan.

One only she knows who can comfort her sorrow,
One who can lighten the gloom of her way;
Surely his light form will come on the morrow,
E'en though he linger and tarry to-day.

END OF CANTO I.

CANTO II.

DARK was the storm—the floods were high;
To torrents rose the mountain rills,
And whirling winds were in the sky,
That flung the clouds against the hills.
By Terek's wave a hunter bold
Stands sternly facing to the wind;
Nought recks he of the rain or cold,
Nor thunder-clouds that roll behind;
His thoughts are bent on such a light,
Or such a form of light and air,
That e'en can make the tempest bright,
And scatters radiance everywhere.

But wretched man ! so often sport of fate !
If morning shine, the eve is desolate ;
The fairest flower the foremost dies away,
Or, e'er it blossoms, withers in decay.

Oh, blighting Time ! thy cold, remorseless hand
With mouldering dust obscures life's crystal sand ;
Wraps all the past in cold oblivion's shroud,
And paints the future like a golden cloud,
That lures us onward with bright visions fair,
Then fades, and leaves us maddened with despair.

Thus, whilst the hunter's fancy fled
From height to height of joy and bliss,
From nuptial feast to bridal bed,
From lover's smile to loving kiss ;
Onward through the glade there went
The trader's motley armament
Of turbaned Turk, and swarthy slave,
And horsemen, whose bright trappings wave
As golden banners in the breeze,
And glitter through the forest trees,
Like those bright birds in ancient story
Whose feathers are a robe of glory.
For hushed was the voice of the blast for a space,
And pale, through the dark gloom, fair Cynthia's face
Cast a soft shadow, or a misty light,
Silvering the turbans of purple and white,
And lightened the diamonds that flashed on the hilt,
Though clouded their rays by the dark stain of guilt.

Just then a wanton gust of air,
That turned and eddied like the tide,
And seemed to scramble everywhere,
Blew, for a transient space, aside
The litter curtain, where there lay
The fairest of the Moslem's prey.

Had a thunderbolt been hurled
From some distant, starry world ;—
Had the moonbeams from on high
Changed to blood's deep crimson dye ;—
Or had all the hosts that dwell
In the darkest caves of hell,
Like myriad locusts o'er the sky
Met the astonished hunter's eye ;—
He had stood unmoved by fear,
Spread they far, or came they near ;
But when all his hopes were laid
On the fair Circassian maid,—
To see her from his power thrust,
And bartered to a dotard's lust,
Numbed his arm and chilled his heart,
Which ceased awhile to act their part ;
A dizzy sickness filled his head,
And left him to all semblance dead.

There is a sad confusion on the brain
When wakening reason comes to us again ;
Old scenes seem new, the new are strange and dread,
And fever throbs through all the aching head ;—

The cheek may flush, and yet the hand is chill ;
The parchéd lip craves water from the rill ;
The light distresses, and the darkness wears ;
Glad thoughts are crushed beneath a weight of cares
Thus when the sun had bronzed the orient gate,
The hunter rose confused and desolate,
Felt some strange trouble, some strong weight oppress,
And mingled thoughts of wrong and bitterness.
Then the whole truth rose dark before his brain,
Like a huge spectre on a haunted plain.

The earth now glowed with every hue ;
Night's curtain, from the darkness rolled,
Had left the sky one sea of blue,—
   The sun a globe of gold :
But had the scene been twice as fair,
Or had the day been bleak and chill,—
Had fragrant balm perfumed the air,
Or thunder rolled above the hill,—
He had not marked it, scarce could say
Whether it were the night or day.
He starts ! an object meets his sight,
Glistening in the morning light.
The warrior knew that gem of yore,
It is the ring that Tsoé wore
On her tapering finger white
When they met the other night.
And whilst he raised it from the ground,
And turned it slowly round and round,

An agéd slave towards him drew,
Carefully eyed him through and through,
Then asked him if he knew who wore
The ring that in his hand he bore.
Then she, weeping, sadly told
How the pensive maid was sold,
And how fast the rosy streak,
Faded from her tear-stained cheek,
And that she had bade her swear
Ne'er to cease from toil and care
Till she found the hunter true,
Who the name of Tsoé knew,
And beg him long, and hard, and late
To save her from her cruel fate.

The hunter waved his sword above,—
A sunbeam kissed it as it rose ;
It seemed a sign of hate and love,
Sunshine and death together close.
He swore the mountain maid to save,
Or find a warrior's early grave—
To meet the Moslem's sabre's blow
With blood for blood, and thrust for thrust,
And see life's parting current flow
From warriors levelled with the dust.
A moment knelt he on the ground,
Suppliant before the Lord of Light,
Then, with a strong determined bound,
In the dark wood he passed from sight.

He is gone ;—his love unbroken,—
His strong desire will not wait ;
And that single precious token
Turns the wavering scales of fate.

He is gone ;—o'er brake and valley,—
He is gone ;—o'er brake and fell.
Will the hunter idly dally
Till he find his lost gazelle ?

He is gone ;—may heaven speed him
Through the troubled waves of life,
Angels to his fair one lead him,
Guard him through the battle strife.

END OF CANTO II.

———◆———

CANTO III.

THERE stands a castle that grimly towers
Among Edessa's shadowy bowers,
And high in air above it rolled
A blood-red flag with cross of gold.
Within its courtyard ringing clear
Was heard the clash of furbished spear,
And many steeds impatient neigh
To gallop to the bloody fray.

Their archéd necks, and trappings bright,
All gorgeous in the morning light—
Gascons, Normans, Celts are standing
Side by side together banding;
Side by side they sternly stand,
Heart with heart, and hand with hand,
Each one harbouring deadly hate
To the ruthless sons of fate,
Who hold the shrine that God has given,
Most rare to earth, most dear to heaven.

And see the Moslems onward come
With cry of war, and roll of drum,
Their folded turbans of many a hue,
Like gems that sparkle, or sunlit dew;
And swift are their chargers, and numerous their hordes,
And keen are their lances, and strong are their swords.
So they advance—on, like the tide,
Which forward rolls on every side
Until some massive cliffs arise
To kiss the azure of the skies,
Then backward rushes with an angry sound,
Confusing the waves with their fierce rebound.

Thus the Moslems staggering reel
When they meet the Christian's steel;
But on again, o'er bodies dead,
Fresh warriors pass with war-cry dread,—

Then flash of arms, and clouds of dust,
And roll of drums, and sabre thrust,
With wild confusion fill the plain,
And slaughter holds her fierce domain.
And now the infidels gain ground ;
Again the Christians, turning round,
Still grimly face towards the foe,
And backward to their fortress go.
But there, a wild impetuous band
Engage the Moslems hand to hand ;
So fierce their charge, so keen their lance,
They stay, and turn the foes' advance.
Champion-like, their leader's blow
Lays many an arméd Tartar low ;
Though his sabre is red with the blood of the slain,
He strikes, and he waves it again and again ;—
No iron plates his limbs enthrall,
But he passes unscathed where thousands fall ;
So light is his form, and so agile his limb,
That they strike at the air when they strike at him.

But oft when man will fight untired,
By hate and glory half inspired,
Night's gathering darkness steals the power away,
And bids the slayer cease awhile to slay.
The avenger turns, whilst all the Christian band
Essay to press the unknown's gory hand ;
And still one question ever to him came,
" Thy name, bold stranger,—tell us now thy name."

He waved his hand,—a silence fell ;—
Each arméd warrior seemed engrossed ;
His wild words cast a voiceless spell
O'er all that mighty mingled host.
" Brethren," he cried, " and all who bear
Christ's holy emblem on your breast,—
Illustrious knights, who proudly wear
The waving plume and gilded crest,—
My name is little known in strife ;
I dwell 'midst mountain, brake, and fen ;
And lead a common hunter's life,
Far distant from the haunts of men.
But hate of Moslem creed and thrall
Induced me hither to repair,
And ever a far distant call
Seems borne towards me on the air ·
For they have stolen the only form
I ever loved on this sad earth,
The only sunbeam 'midst the storm
That has pursued me from my birth.
And now a solemn vow is mine,
To save her from her cruel lord,
To tear the Moslem from his shrine,
And lay him prostrate on the sward.
Few are my comrades, but when zeal
Uprears the standard of my band,
Keenly falls our ready steel,
Heavy is our willing hand.
Onward I to-night will go,—
And, if heaven will, surprise,

Destroy, and scatter all the foe,
Ere morning flushes in the skies.
In the darkness of the night
Thousands may be slain by ten,
Thousands may be put to flight,
Never to return again.
Adieu ! brave Christians, I'll away,
And fall or combat to the last ;
I cannot rest a single day ;
The page is turned—the die is cast.
I start upon my deadly raid,
To save the unprotected maid,
Or dye the earth with Ronald's blood,
And red the crystal of the flood."

He ceased ;—approving murmurs ran
From knight to knight, from man to man ;
Then rose a wild, tumultuous cry,
That echoed where the rocks were riven,
And upward, swelling to the sky,
Died in the starry vault of heaven.
Then many a knight and warrior went
To join in Ronald's armament ;
Stealthily their path they tread
O'er mingled heaps of unburied dead,
To where the watch-fires gleaming bright
Proclaimed the Moslem's camp that night.

O Hope ! thou dear deluder of the brain !
How false thy promises ! thy words how vain !

Like the deep swamp, that decked with many a bloom
Would lead us onward to a treacherous tomb ;
Its velvet verdure, of an emerald hue,
Conceals its dangerous qualities from view,
Tempts us to venture, then with gurgling flow
Engulfs us in the sepulchre below.
  Thus Ronald's hopes received a blight,
  For when he reached the Moslem host
  He found them well prepared to fight,
. And arméd men from post to post.
  Then all his band were backward driven
  Like leaves before the winds of heaven,
  And he, left lonely 'mid the slain,
  Stood sad and wounded on the plain.

Whole heaps of killed were round him, and above
The stars looked down in silent, mournful love ;
The ghastly faces of the dead were white,
Enveloped in the sable folds of night,
Save where the clotted blood was purpling o'er
The cheek it warmed and flushed an hour before.
Far happier they who perish where they fall,
Than they whose lingering lives give power to crawl,
Who, worn with pain, and faint from loss of blood,
Hear the far murmurs of the distant flood,
Which like some mocking phantom thrice accursed
With laughing ripple goads the pangs of thirst.

Through such a scene passed Ronald, calm and slow,
To outward gaze unmoved by sights of woe,

Till, gasping out its life with piteous cry,
His favourite staghound met his misty eye;
It writhed in agony, and yet essayed
To lick the master's hand, who quickly stayed
The gushing of the wound; but all too late,—
Quivering it fell, and left him desolate.
When fortune blows adverse with fickle blast,
How sweet is each reminder of the past !
E'en though 'tis but a blossom of the earth,
Or some poor brute, to man of little worth,—
Yet to the owner—oh, how fondly dear,
Lives that reminder of a brighter year !
Thus gazing on its dim and closing eye,
The warrior mused distressed and mournfully :
" Is this thy fate, poor creature, this thy end ?
Alas ! in thee, I lose my firmest friend.
Though dumb, thine eye's intelligence and grace
Could read each meaning passing o'er my face.
War, thou grim foe to liberty and art !
The sport of faction, and the game of kings !
Thou numb'st the noblest feelings of the heart,
And mak'st man worse than brutes or common things ;
Thy grandeur is the tawdry banner's wave,
Thy glory is the glory of the grave ! "

Thus musing, Ronald left that scene of woe ;
But where to wander, whither now to go
He recked not ; yet the magic hand of fate
Led him towards that glittering city's gate,

Where pent within the gilded Harem wall
Helpless was she, his hope—his life—his all.

Beside a temple crumbling into earth,
And browned by many a year of sun and dearth,
He paused awhile to rest his steed, and gaze
Upon the city, lit by morning's rays.
The lofty pines, with waving plumes of green,
Give life and verdure to the silent scene ;
The orange flowers with fragrance fill the breeze
That murmurs through the garlands of the trees;
The sunbeams rise upon the crystal foam
Of founts that, gushing from some gilded dome,
Run through the valleys with a laughing sound,
Twining in countless eddies round and round.
And the last dewdrop leaves the blushing rose
Ere wakes Damascus from her night's repose.

But whilst he gazed, a voice came sad and clear
Amid the slumbering stillness of the morn,
And ever coming nearer and more near
Upon the breeze, its plaintive notes were borne;
Starting, he gazed where the grey olives lie,
And strange was the scene that broke on his eye :
    A maiden to the temple fled,
    Her locks wide streaming in the wind ;
    With twisted turban on his head,
    A Moslem rode not far behind.

" For love of Allah," cried the maid,
" I pray thee give me speedy aid,
Else ere this evening I shall be
For ever mate to misery.
My father sold me as his right,—
He sold me to a trader stern ;—
I fly, and one pursues my flight
Who vows that ere he shall return,
Ere night shall veil that ball of fire,
I shall be slave to his desire."
Scarce had she ceased her plaintive cry,
When like a trumpet spake the Turk
In accents fierce, and stern, and high :
" Shouldst thou attempt to draw thy dirk,
Thy flesh shall fust within this place,
A death's head lie, where lies thy face,
And all that wander by shall cry,
'Twas here the Chief of Ajemi
Slew the rash boy that dared to sever
His lawful prey,—his, his for ever."

The hunter answered not a word,
But mounted on his charger light,
Unsheathed his brand, and swiftly spurred,
As spurs a warrior to the fight.
They meet ;—they close with mutual hate and rage—
Advance—retreat—strike—parry—and engage ;
The chargers fall, yet still the riders stand
With foot to foot, and hand engaged to hand,

Till from his wounds the Moslem dropped and died,
And the brave Frank lay bleeding at his side.

As boundeth from some mountain dell
The young and tender-eyed gazelle,
When first it hears the hunter's horn
Ring through the brachen and the thorn;
So when young Ronald bleeding lay,
Faint from the buffets of the fray,
The maiden, springing to his side,
Essayed to quench the ebbing tide
That, ever streaming from the wound,
With scarlet dyed the verdant ground.
From earth she raised the drooping head,
And gazed upon the closing eye;
And from her bosom stole a sigh—
A sigh that might awake the dead.

Her lovely gaze was sad and meek;
The tears that melted in her eye
Were blended with the darker dye
Of feverish glow upon her cheek.

Her russet hair, that downward fell,
Dishevelled, from the golden braid,—
Her words that gentle murmurings made,
Like music from some distant bell,—

All told their tale of nights of woe,
Of days of sorrow and despair,

That make soft beauty sadly fair,
And paint it with a hectic glow.

And as she sat, and wept, and prayed,
Beside the hunter's prostrate form,
Like sunbeams glittering after storm,
Sweet music floated through the glade,
As though some morning chimes were ringing,
And sweetly with the psaltery blending,
Or like a choir of angels singing,
From Eden's verdant groves descending.

And the maiden gazed on his prostrate form,
Till passed o'er her face a sudden storm
Of red and of pale, of smiles and tears,
Of joy and of pain, of hopes and fears.
     She placed her hand upon his brow ;
     He started when he heard her sigh,
     And faintly whispering Tsoé's name,
     Rose from his swoon of agony.

Then, in a long, long clasp, that telleth
     Love lies deep in either's heart,
And in each tender feeling dwelleth,
     Twining coils in every part,
Tsoé finds once more the dearest
     Idol of her youthful breast,
He who ever should be nearest,
     He who ever should be best.

A fragrant bower beside them stood,
With almond tree and sandal wood;
Within its cool and leafy shade
Concealed, the warrior and the maid
Passed all that long and sunny day;
At night they softly stole away,
Together journeying, hand in hand,
Towards Edessa's friendly land,
United by a stronger plight,
Than broken ring or trothal rite,—
A firm and sacred promise given,
Beneath the cloudless eye of heaven.

*　　　*　　　*　　　*

Now has dawned the marriage day;
Leave them in each other's love;
Love ungazed on loves the best—
Angels watching from above.

Crystal drops, that softly break,
Break and glitter into light;
Cradled in the lily's breast,
Lit by morning sunbeams bright.

Violets, that hide to kiss
Dewdrops of the blushing morn,
Raise your purple eyes, and gaze
Up through the broken thorn.

Birds, that carol in the grove,
Birds, that warble all the day,
Tune your voices to my song,
Tune your measure to my lay.

Children, raise your large full eyes,
Homes at once of smile and tear;
Clap your rosy little hands,
Sing my song both far and near.

Angels, singing in the stars,
Sound the nuptials through the sky;
Singing in the fields of light,
Shout the glad news far and high.

POMPÉII.

D

POMPEII.

I.

POMPEII! As I stand within thy wall,
　　And view the fragments of thy brighter day,
Think on thy grandeur—then thy sudden fall,
See thy fair columns wasted by decay,—
No limpid waters sparkle in thy fount,
Nor frost each sunbeam with their ceaseless foam;
To thy high temple may the stranger mount,
Or wander through the burgher's empty home,
That formed in one short day his dwelling-place and
　　tomb.

II.

Unrivalled is the scene that meets the eye
From every turning of thy narrow street,—
The cloudless azure of Italia's sky,
Tyrrhenian's waters slumbering at thy feet;
Behind thee, steeped in floods of purple light,
Vesuvius rears to heaven his sterile crest,
Or, in the stillness of a southern night,
Casts quenchless fire from his troubled breast,
Whose ever-restless surgings have no need of rest.

III.

Far to the north, queen of the lovely bay,
Proud Naples rears her battlements on high ;
And as they catch the sun's declining ray
Reflect the gorgeous colouring of the sky ;
But when he sinks behind the crested wave,
Bearing to other climes his welcome light,
Then, like the marble o'er the silent grave,
Each battlement and rampart pale to white,   ·
As fades the fragile bud when chilled by dreary night.

IV.

But thou art reft of all that once was fair,
Save the gay frescoes on thy roofless walls,
Which seem to mock the horrible despair
That haunts each corner of thy noiseless halls.
Here stands a jester in a motley coat,
Stretching his hands towards the grinning crowd ;
There sports a Satyr, or a bearded goat,
Unscathéd by the overspreading cloud,
Which swiftly formed for thee pall, sepulchre, and
      shroud.

V.

Thy floors are paved with tesselated stone,
Or fretted marble of the richest hue ;
Thy fluted columns, headless and alone,
Are stained with crimson or imperial blue ;
Thy streets no more are worn by chariots gay ;

No horsemen enter at thy open gate,
But every stone is crusted with decay,
And tells the story of thy hopeless fate ;
Oh, lone Pompeii ! thou art sadly desolate.

VI.

The main, that in the prosperous days of yore
With plaintive murmurs lulled thy sons to rest,
No longer woos thy uninviting shore,
Nor rocks thy galleys on its troubled breast ;*
Now, where its waters fling their hoary spray,
The sombre olive and the orange bloom
O'er spreading vine, and prickly cactus gay,
And form a garden round thy ashy tomb,
Like wandering sunbeams breaking devastation's
    gloom.

VII.

Historians with their magic pens have told,
And poets sung it in heroic lay,
That thou wast prosperous in the days of old,
When Cæsar ruled thee with imperial sway ;
But thou wast doomed, not to the slow decay
Which other cities of thy time have known,—
In one short hour thy glory passed away,
And left thee withered, blighted, and alone,
Unroofed thy dwellings, and destroyed thy walls of
    stone.

* Pompeii, whose walls were once washed by the sea, is now about a mile distant.

VIII.

Ah ! happy they who fell without a cry—
With scarce a moment to bewail their fate ;
One instant wrung with throbbing agony,
The next o'erwhelmed by a crushing weight
Of seething rocks, hurled from the gates of night,
Causing destruction in their maddening fall,—
A cloud of melting ashes in their flight,
Covering the city like a funeral pall,*
Whilst trembling earth beneath rent the embattled
    wall. †

IX.

E'en now are ashes of a human mould,
Blackened with age, and terrible to see ;—
A miser grasping still the yellow gold,
Hard by his side a coffer's ponderous key.
Within that niche what form arrests the eye,—
Erect and ghastly as a midnight ghost ?
A soldier who hath scorned to hide or fly,
And perished like a hero at his post, ‡
'Midst clouds of monstrous form, like hell's accurséd
    host. †

* Pompeii was overwhelmed by showers of scoriæ, pumice, and ashes.

† The town was shaken during the eruption by violent earthquakes.

‡ A man with a bag of gold, and a soldier guarding the gate in full armour, are among the skeletons that have been found.

§ Dion Cassius mentions strange hissing noises from the ground, and the monstrous shapes assumed by the clouds, which seemed like infernal agents of destruction and death.

X.

Lo ! pause.—A female form lies tombless there,
No longer gay and lovely to behold.
Where now those graceful streams of waving hair
That caught each sunbeam in a web of gold?
Within those sockets once were eyes whose bend
Might rouse to fire or chill the lover's heart ;
Fair smiles and tears together softly blend
With all the witchcraft of a woman's art ;—
And think,—this clay hath lived, hath loved, hath
    played its part.

XI.

But there were those, in dungeons dark and drear,
Without one hope, one penetrating ray :
In ceaseless darkness and delirious fear
They gnawed their chains, and wasted day by day.
E'en now they lie, though stifled are their groans,
Upon the dungeon's damp and mildewed floor ;
The cankering chains have rusted to their bones ;*
A jailor standeth at the ponderous door,—
And dead keep dead in death, as life watched life
    before.

XII.

O, great arena ! † as. I gaze on thee,
And view the shadow of thy ancient mould,

* In the prisons, skeletons were found with rusty chains still
clinging to them.
† Dion Cassius relates that the citizens were assembled in the
Amphitheatre at the time of the eruption.

A fleeting vision stealeth over me,
A dream of what thou wast in years of old,
When all thy terraces were crowded high
With Romans, Greeks, and many a swarthy slave;
Thy centre awned, to shield from sunny sky,
And like the thunder of Tyrrhenian's wave,
Shout followed shout, as passed each victim to his
    grave.

XIII.

Within the centre of that great array,
A gladiator firmly takes his stand;
He knows the sunset of that fated day
May find him lifeless on the scattered sand,
So grasps his dirk with more than mortal air,
And stands erect, immovable as stone,
For what gives wilder courage than despair?
More self-reliance than to feel alone,—
One sheltering arm to save,—and know that arm your
    own?

XIV.

In yon low dungeon, where the whitening bones
Lie crumbling in a dry and sure decay,
Methought I heard the lion's restless groans
To spring with fury on his human prey.
The gates are opened, and with savage roar
He flies to meet the calm, expecting foe;
Such foe the beast had seldom met before,
Ne'er felt the weight of such a crushing blow;
He stops,—he wheels,—he stays,—and then again
    stoops low.

XV.

Fast from his side the purple stream flows free,
And mingles with the cold and yellow sand;
His eyes are fixed in vengeful agony
Upon the hated wielder of that brand.
He rears,—he springs,—he flies to meet his foe,
And bears him backward with a crushing weight;
Yet still his breast receives another blow;
The balance trembles in the hand of fate,
And all that bending crowd in breathless silence wait.

XVI.

Now rolling, struggling, on the ground they lie,—
They strike, they tear, they grapple, and they maim;
Fast flows the blood, yet each will win or die,
The brute for carnage, and the man for fame.
But hark! what solemn sound arrests the ear?
What sudden darkness overspreads the sky?
The beast has crouched in wonder and in fear,—
The gladiator stands bewildered by,—
Whilst from that great array breaks forth a thrilling cry.

XVII.

They rush in wild confusion from the place,
And gaze in wonder at the dreadful sight;
Fear chases colour from each upturned face,
And makes it ghastly in the changing light;
For from Vesuvius glares that warning star—

A spreading tree of ashes and of flame,*
That shoots its scorching branches wide and far ;
Its fiery fruits th' approaching doom proclaim,
And quell each startled eye, and shake each stalwart
    frame. †

XVIII.

And there was death, and every form of woe
That shatters reason and disturbs the brain ;
Fierce flame above, and trembling earth below,—
Darkness on earth, and trouble on the main ;
Rocks falling, hot with years of scorching flame,
And lava streaming from the burning mount,
Whilst ceaseless thunder from its centre came,
And sulphurous waters from its restless fount,
And countless desolations, pen can ne'er recount.

XIX.

The houses reel, untimely night hath spread
Her sable curtain o'er the trembling plain ;
The old have hidden, and the young have fled ;
The thief still lingers in the hope of gain.‡

* "I cannot give you a more exact description of its figure
than by resembling it to that of a pine tree, for it shot up a great
height in the form of a trunk, and extended itself at the top in
sort of branches."—PLINY.

† "He was now so near the mountain that the cinders, which
grew thicker and hotter, fell into the ship, together with black
pieces of burning rock."—PLINY.

‡ In the temple of Isis, a skeleton was found with a bag of
money in the hand.

Vain plunder ! for when hell hath waxen bold,
And vowed destruction on our mortal race,
How brittle is the cable formed of gold !
Can man bribe mountains with its gilded face,
Or buy in other worlds an everlasting place ?

XX.

Accurséd metal !—yet for thee men brave
Soul, body, all that they can call their own ;
Will rob the sacred precincts of the grave,
And rouse its inmate for the precious stone ;
And when possessed, it rusteth in the heart,
And chafes the conscience with a restless woe,
Though, gilded be the tomb with every art,
A loathsome skeleton is viewed below,—
Worms and decay within,—without, an empty show.

XXI.

From Isis' temple rings a piercing cry ;
The victim quivers on the sacred sod ;—
Yet sculptured stone was their cold deity !
The chisel was the maker of their god !
Would Mars throw down his pike and helmet
	bright,
Jove cease his thunderings for that kneeling band,
Would Venus stay her dove-drawn chariot's flight,
The Furies quench their thrice-accurséd brand,
To save from hovering death a strip of peopled land ?

XXII.

Yet still they pray, whilst boiling waters pour
Like seething cataracts upon the land ; *
The main affrighted starteth from the shore,
And leaves its inmates on the writhing sand.†
Another crash, that shakes the trembling air,—
Another burst of pale and livid light, —
Another cry,—another stifled prayer,—
A pause,—and then—a dark and ashy blight ;
One piercing, thrilling shriek, and then—eternal night.

XXIII.

'Twas thus that busy fancy phantoms drew,
And when I raised from earth my downcast eye,
Each changing vision faded from my view,
And left me gazing long on vacancy ;
But as the misty clouds of morning fly
Confused before the rude and driving blast,
Clear rose the mountains and the cloudless sky
Like some fair vision of the glorious past,
Whilst sunset over all its golden mantle cast.

XXIV.

I wander to the Street of Tombs, and view
The burial-places of the buried town ;

* Scalding water fell in torrents during the eruption.
† " The sea seemed to roll back upon itself, and to be drive
from its banks by the convulsive motion of the earth ; and man
sea animals were left upon its shore, from which the water ha
receded."—PLINY.

Mosaics and marbles of a bronzéd hue
Adorn the sepulchres of old renown ;
The circling laurel marks the hero's grave ;—
But who that hero ? where his battles won ?
Was he a rover of the restless wave ?
Or sought he glory 'neath a foreign sun ?
Life, name, and memory,—all save burial-place are
    gone.

XXV.

The day had sunk to eve, the eve had passed
In the short twilight of a southern land ;
Long through those streets I wandered, till at last
Dark walls encircled me on either hand,
And I was in a vault—a vault whose wall.
Was moulded by the finger of decay,*
For where the trembling beams of Cynthia fall
There stands a grim and horrible array,—
Forms human, though not flesh, once more returned
    to clay.

XXVI.

A long gaunt row of skeletons they stand,
And numb the gazer with an icy chill ;
Corruption passes o'er each crumbling hand,
Where, in cold mockery, clings the diamond still.

* The impression of part of a woman's figure is still seen in
the clay that has hardened against the wall in the vault below the
house of Diomede, where seventeen skeletons, or rather bodies
of clay, were found—rings still encircling the fingers of one of
the figures, supposed to be that of the mistress of the house.

Yes ! gems may make the beautiful more fair ;
The brow seems purer 'neath a pearly wreath ;
But oh, what satire flashes from their glare
When coupled with the rusty scythe of death,
No longer frosted by the gentle dews of breath !

XXVII.

But I must leave thee, City of the Dead,
The grave of thousands, mother of decay,—
A mausoleum, wrapt in silent dread
O'er the weird remnants of forgotten clay.
Farewell ! I must no longer linger here,
Nor dream I see thee as in years gone by ;
Thy memory claims a sympathizing tear,—
Thy fate demands the tribute of a sigh,
Which even stone to stone were stony to deny.

GARDEN MELODIES.

GARDEN MELODIES.

SHOWERS.

SOFT summer showers enrich the flowers,
    And swell the murmuring stream,
Refresh the air with odours fair,
    And make the land to teem
With emerald grass, and lilies tall,
With rushing brook, and waterfall.

They step on the ridge of the rainbow bridge,
    And leap o'er its glowing side,
Or, wrapt in the cloud for a sail and shroud,
    On the breast of whirlwinds ride ;
Then fall in ice, and rain, and snow,
To beautify the earth below.

They water the dell of the wild gazelle,
    And brighten its languid eye,
And gem its hair with raindrops fair,
    As they gleam and glitter by,
Till it gaily springs from bower to bower.
In welcome of the freshening shower.

E

They gladden the glad, and cheer the sad,
 And blend with the mourner's tear ;
Steal through the veil to the forehead pale,
 And bid the drooping cheer ;
They cool the air o'er the feverish bed,
Loving the living, and weeping the dead.

THE FOUNTAIN.

BRIGHT in the light of the noonday's sun
 The fountain flings its spray,
Like a crystal gem in a diadem
 It holds each varied ray ;
Its gay drops sparkle, and glitter, and break,
And ripple along by the sunny lake.

Now, like rubies of ruddy hue,
 They melt into the stream,
Like orange flowers in shady bowers,
 Like a silvered meteor's beam ;
Then, like a shower of emeralds fall,
Green as the moss on the garden wall.

And the golden fish around it play,
 The lilies around it grow,
So pure and sweet, where the waters meet,
 And white as the mountain snow ;
Like a maiden that sits all silent and pale,
When her true lover's bark is tossed by the gale.

So ever may the joys of life
   Flow on through sunny years;
No furrows of time, no sin, no crime,
   No shedding of sorrow's tears;
But scattering the gems of friendship and love,
Till gemlike we shine in the kingdom above.

RED AND WHITE ROSES.

THERE, with the pearly dew of morn,
   Two lovely roses stand;
They are stripped by the same cold winter,
   They are clothed by spring's fair hand;
And as that season rolls away,
The summer gives them blossoms gay.

To one it gives the paler hue
   That lilies love to wear,
The very type of chastity,
   A gem for maiden's hair;
By hope's fond kiss the other flushed,
Glanced at true love, and softly blushed.

Yet once in deadly civil strife
   These rival blossoms vied;
The paler blanched the crimson white,
   The white with gore was dyed;

Till o'er proud Tudor's bridal bed,
Red kissed the pale, and pale the red.

Oft have they decked the coffin lid,
 And the bride on the bridal morn ;
And the wandering tear they have often chid
 From the cheek that care hath worn ;
And e'en, like watchful angels, bloom
On the cold bosom of the tomb.

THE GENTIAN.

FREE and fresh are the Alpine flowers that blow
 'Midst the rugged rock and the summer snow ;
Unscathed by the chill and the mountain blast,
Uncrushed by the avalanche rushing past :
Sleeping serene, as a bird in its nest,
On the icefield's cold and joyless breast.

The hoar-frost binds them in a crystal net,
And, like fair sapphires amidst diamonds set,
Their blue corollas, still true and bright,
Adorn the diadem of Jura's height ;
Telling their tale to the dwellers below,
That love may rest calm in the midst of the snow.

THE DAISY.

THE daisy lies, and looks to the skies,
   On the lawn beside the lake;
Sealed all night by its petals white,
   Which no rude hand shall break
Till morning's young and ruddy ray
Has blushed into the perfect day.

And the dewdrops rest upon its breast,
   Like gems on a golden cup;
And the leaves unfurled, like edges pearled,
   To the azure sky look up;
And each white ray with coral is tipped,
As if in sunlight it were dipped.

And children play through the livelong day,
   With laughter and with song,
And deck their hair with its blossoms fair,
   As they merrily trip along;
And the aged sigh, and sigh in vain,
For the pleasures linked in the daisy chain.

LILIA.

FAIR is my lawn with many a flower;
   Rare are the shrubs in my woody bower;
And the crystal fountain with its play
Cools the still lake from day to day.

But there shines an eye more calm and clear
Than the sparkling streams of my fairy mere ;
And a cheek that rivals in its bloom
The blushing rose on the baby's tomb.

And there rings a voice as soft and free
As ever angel voice can be ;
And there heaves a bosom pure and white
As lilies that shine by the pale moonlight ;
For Lilia is the brightest and sweetest bud
That glides o'er my lawn, or rests by my flood.

See her, when the morn is bright,
Tripping with a gay delight,
O'er the turf, and mead, and flower,
Laughing in the garden bower !

See her, by the cool fresh lake,
Where the sunny ripples break,
Watch the golden fishes play,
Glittering 'neath the fountain's spray !

See her when the sun reposes,
Midst the fresh and fragrant roses,
Like a form from Eden bless'd,
Ever actively at rest !

Not a thought of care or sorrow,—
Sunshine cometh with to-morrow,—
Trusting, loving, sin forgiven,
Finding earth as sweet as heaven !

THE FALL OF JERUSALEM.

THE FALL OF JERUSALEM.

O LAND of Israel! once so proudly fair!
Thy woods were palm-groves, incense was thine
air!
O'erthrown thou standest like some broken shrine;
Thy crumbling fragments lovely in decline!
Blue is thy lake as when its waves were trod
By thy once suffering, still rejected God!
But where thy cities now?   The rose may bloom
In mournful loveliness above their tomb,
Or the lean wolf in savage hunger roam
Over the unknown thresholds of thy home!
Jerusalem! who mark thy bulwarks now?
Or where thy temple crowning Zion's brow,—
That fane which thou rejoicedst in of old,
Which Gentiles wondering trembled to behold?
Where now thy courts once filled with heavenly light,—
Thy priests arrayed in sacerdotal white?
All have to dust—to trodden dust returned;
Thy sons are slain—thy holy temple burned.
    Thou queenly city! throned amidst the hills!
Now crushed beneath the weight of countless ills!
Wasted by age! blighted by Roman sword!
Thy grave the dwelling of a Turkish horde!

Thy temple by a Moslem mosque entombed !
Thy bulwarks broken, and thy towers doomed !
Jerusalem ! why are thy sons oppressed ?
Why broken, restless, can they find no rest ?

*   *   *   *

The sun resplendent rose o'er Zion's height,
Bathing its gilded dome with rosy light,
And with its gay beams kissed the dew away,
The pearly offspring of the curtained day ;
But oft when joyous nature casts her smiles
O'er lofty hills and groups of sea-girt isles,
O'er verdant pasture, or clear crystal lake,
The deadly feuds of men her calm spell break ;
Thus, as fair daylight climbs the azure vault,
The Hebrew wakes to death, and dread assault ;
For Ariel groans 'neath famine's withering hand,
And Roman legions devastate the land.
Yet 'midst the clouds, that curled ascend the sky,
The temple stands in queenlike majesty,
Calmly amid the desolating storm
That sweeps around her fair though lonely form,
E'en as a stray palm in the desert stands,
Majestic 'midst a sea of burning sands.
Loud from the fated city rings the cry
Of those who die, and those who fear to die ;
Whilst goaded into madness by despair,
Some shout revenge, and others wildly tear
The dry, sere skin from off their mangled bones,
And fill the air with rending shrieks and groans ;

Whilst pale men on their care-chased faces fall,
And for the Son of David vainly call.
Then wading through the stream of slippery gore
The Roman legions in confusion pour,
And still they wave their falchions o'er their head,
As each winged moment marks fresh warriors dead.

O Ariel! what confusion reigns in thee!
Thy temple burns; thy stalwart soldiers flee—
Flee to the courts, where leaps the fulgent flame,
And in their burning bosom burial claim.
For now is desolation Judah's king,
And from thy flaming shrine is heard the ring
Of arms upon the tesselated stone,
As each proud Rabbi gasps his parting groan.

Night soon her curtain casts upon the scene,
Hiding the city 'neath a sable screen,
Like unto ebony with diamonds stud,
Engirded with a faintly tingéd flood
Of rosy light, flung from the sun's last ray,
A blushing remnant of the parting day.
But in the spangled pall that nature spread
Were strange intruders, that had swiftly sped
From the far realms of vast ethereal space,
To find o'er Salem's pyre a dwelling-place,
And view the conflagration of the fane,
Which tinged with lurid glare their far domain.
But now the wild flames wildly burst anew,
And tinge the marble towers with ruby hue,
Wrapping the sanctuary in lurid cloud,
Which, like a spectre in his fiery shroud,

Stands fierce among the prone and prostrate dead,
Chasing forth pallor by a hectic red,
And lighting up the gloomy, glazéd eyes
Of those who writhe in death's last agonies.
    So Judah fell,—fell 'neath that city's yoke,
Which Carthage conquered, Grecia's power broke,
Whose eagles swept o'er land, o'er foaming sea ;
Her strength to God a tool,—to man a mystery.

*   *   *   *

Jerusalem ! in thy dread doom I see
The living truth of sacred prophecy ;
For when with tearful eye the Christ divine
From Olivet beheld thy marble shrine,—
Thy golden towers, like vassal suns, that throw
O'er minor spheres their tributary glow,—
He with omniscient gaze did sadly see
Through the dark veil of hidden destiny,
And wept that thou thro' countless years shouldst
    stand
A scornéd stranger in a stranger's land ;—
He wept the vengeance that should visit thee,
And mourned thy long and drear captivity.
Yet e'en through judgment beaming mercy shone,
And thou, O Zion ! blighted, withered, lone,
Shalt like the Phœnix from thine ashes rise,
And live beneath the smile of Paradise.
Thy sons again shall dress fair Carmel's vine,
Thy dark-eyed daughters in their tresses twine

The blushing blossoms of sweet Sharon's rose,
And pluck the lilies where the Jordan flows.
Then He who bore a thorny crown for them,
Shall ever bear Jehovah's diadem,
And as their conquering King shall joy to see
His ransomed people dwell in unity ;
Whilst all the wondering nations of the earth
Shall sing the greatness of thy second birth.
Jerusalem ! of all thy glories reft,
Hope is the only anchor to thy children left !

A LEGEND OF
PRINCE ALPHONSO.

A LEGEND OF

PRINCE ALPHONSO.

I.

THERE stern Ferrara rears on high
  Her battlements and ramparts fair,
That cast their shadows everywhere,
And pierce into the midnight sky.

And siege and storm those towers have seen,
And many a shock those dark walls know;
Deep, dreary dungeons lie below,
All damp with fungus wet and green.

The light that falls upon their floor
Seems like a prisoner from the day,
That, if it could, would run away,
And leave things darker than before.

II.

A moat encircles all the keep;
A drawbridge o'er the moat is thrown,
Resting upon a ponderous stone,
And 'neath it blackened waters sleep.

F

Oft o'er that drawbridge rang the tread
Of arméd men, and archers light,
Who passed into the silent night
With weapons keen, and banners spread.

III.

'Twas such a troop that left the quay
And wound along the banks of Po,
Whose ever-eddying waters flow
In laughing ripples to the sea.

Alphonso rode amid the band,
But only for a little way ;
The timorous Duke had bade him stay,
A tacit dweller in the land.

Yet he was young, and strong, and brave,
And longed to hear the battle's roar,
And by each pope and saint he swore
That Spain should see his banners wave.

But cooling as he onward went,
He drew unnoticed from the band,
And curbed his steed, and sheathed his brand,
And to the town his path he bent.

IV.

A chapel stood on banks of Po,
And none would enter it by night,
For legends said that elf and sprite
Held revel in the vaults below.

Alphonso, as he homeward sped
In angry murmurings at his woe,
" Since Spain my courage may not know,
I'll throw my gauntlet to the dead."

He entered at the open door,
Then trod the drear and grave-sown aisle,
And set to muse a little while
Upon the glorious days of yore.

v.

A moonbeam, wandering from the rest,
Bright throught the Gothic windows shone,
And fell upon the altar stone,
And tinged the plate and chalice blest.

And then, with chant and solemn tread,
Bald priests come wandering through the night,
And choristers in cassocks white,
The spectres of forgotten dead.

They glided to each vacant chair,
And kindled many a taper bright,
That shed a pure and peaceful light
O'er broidered stole and surplice fair.

And as they waved the sacred fire,
He heard a gentle, distant strain ;
It ceased ; and then it woke again,
A low soft "Ave, ave Maria."

And then there issued from the gloom,
In sombre garbs and hoods of snow,
And eyes that patient suffering show,
The nuns that slumbered in the tomb.

VI.

Up rose the Prince, and bowed his head,
And turned towards the open door;
His scabbard fell upon the floor,
And rang among the restless dead.

And at that sound, they murmured low,
And glided wildly everywhere,
And then they faded into air,
Like waters 'neath the sunbeam's glow.

VII.

Alphonso left the church in fear;
The moon upon the earth had stepped
Where it had shone; a planet crept
To see it sink into the mere.

Clear rays of silver gemmed with dew,
Bright pathways linking sky with earth,
Returning where they had their birth,
Through the dark vault of heavens blue.

And then the waters caught the light,
The ripples piped along the shore,
And fiercely waged their mimic war
'Gainst bending reed and lily bright.

VIII.

A spirit floated from above,
And rested on the waters clear,
And plucked a lily from the mere,
And wrote upon it, *"God is love."*

Her form was of angelic mould,
Unclouded beauty in her eye,
Which told its tale of purity,
Through the light veil of tresses gold.

IX.

On her fair bosom lay a dove ;
Her radiance filled the rustling trees,
And love was whispered by the breeze,
And stream and valley echoed love.

A spotless dove, with silver wing,
Pure as the bosom where it lay,
That never wished to fly away,
But ever there would rest and sing.

And in a measure strange and new,
A psalm of heavenly tune it sung,
For magic birds have magic tongue,
And sometimes human voices too.

SONG OF THE DOVE.*

Mourn not the loss of warfare's glory,
  When valiant foes must yield ;
Repine not for the honours gory
  Of the blood-red Spanish field.

* The "Song of the Dove" is written by a friend.

There is an enemy that stalketh,
  O'er fields that are not red ;
There is a conqueror that walketh
  Not o'er the gruesome dead.

For oft the poor and simple crieth
  Within the city wall ;
And oft the broken-hearted sigheth
  Beneath oppression's thrall.

And there dark ignorance is rampant,
  And wickedness is rife ;
There fierce flames, spreading fresh and lambent,
  Consume the springs of life.

And no one passeth through the city
  In panoply of love ;
No one to cast the eye of pity,
  And raise the hope above.

Then be the conqueror that walketh
  Not o'er the gruesome dead ;
Go, fight the enemy that stalketh
  O'er fields that are not red.

*   *   *   *

X.

Clear was the song, and every note
Was echoed from the chapel wall ;
And then they seemed to sink and fall,
To join the ripples as they float.

How soft the carol of the bird !
Untutored music is more sweet
Than rules confined and measured beat,—
It soars above the common herd.

The lark springs from her grassy bed,
And melts into the liquid sky ;
And then it seems to float on high,
And scatters blessings on your head.

XI.

'Twas thus the sweet bird's sympathy
Unloosed the chains which anger bound ;
It made the chords of hope resound,
And woke the man to energy.

And whilst he wondered hereupon,
And gazed towards the spirit fair,
A cloud came floating through the air,
Enveloped her, and she was gone.

And then the rosy line of dawn
Paled all the planets of the sky ;
And now they seem to melt and die,
As dewdrops melt upon the lawn.

So fair at morn is every sphere,
It seems as though to man were given
A fleeting dream—a peep of heaven,
To make him feel the world less drear.

From Nature's hand, from Nature's voice,
Men read and learn what they should do,
And when they read her teachings through,
Perceive their beauty, and rejoice.

Calmed by the visions of his sleep,
Instructed by the word they bore,
He left the shallows by the shore
And launched into the unknown deep.

He breasted manfully the wave
Of famine, fever, toil, and care ;
Dispersed the fetid, poisoned air
That rose around him from the grave.

The poor men blessed him far and nigh,
And poets praised him in their lays,
And aged folk recalled the days—
Those happy days of charity.

HISTORICAL PIECES.

HISTORICAL PIECES.

THE DRUID.

'Twas midnight ;—
And the wintry wind groaned through the forest,
In whose groves I saw—or thought I saw—Death.
Grim was his visage, and his sapless bones
Creaked like the branch whereon he held himself,
Whilst his rotting teeth were chattering grimly
In the cold and wintry wind.

I turned me from this hideous King of Night,
When lo ! a sight more horrid met my gaze.
A mother clasping in her arms a child
She sought to save from one who, clothed in white,
Wore round his brow a crown of faded oak,
And held within his hand a double knife.
His arm was bared, and raised as though to strike
The heart of her who at his feet lay low.
She might have been a queen, for well I wot
A diadem ne'er circled fairer brows ;
Nor 'neath a gem more pleading eyes found place

Than those which sought to change his savage mood,
And save her child and self from early death.
" Help, help," she cried; and from her eyes rolled tears,
Those silent messengers of woman's woe
That iron melt, when beauty lets them flow.
One lovely hand held fast the Druid's robe,
The other clasped the infant to her heart.
Could man look on such grief and not be moved ?
Would God accept an offering half so dear?
But he is neither God nor man to know
That pity is a gift more truly great
Than sacrifice or offerings ere can be,—
And so—to please the gods that rule the land—
In guiltless blood he bathed his guilty hand.

EDWY'S ADDRESS TO ELGIVA.

WOULD that I once more might clasp thee
    To my aching widow'd heart ;
Once more feel thine arms around me,
    Then 'twould be less hard to part.

Had I seen thee slowly drooping
    To the grave, where all must go ;
O'er thy couch in sorrow stooping,
    Watch'd thy roses fade to snow ;

Then I might, though crush'd with sorrow,
   Still have borne against the blow—
Gathering strength from every morrow,
   Wreak'd revenge upon my foe.

But in malice thou wast taken
   From the shelter of my arms;
Scathed by fire, and forsaken,
   Yet they could not spoil thy charms,

Till, in rage's hideous madness
   At thy never-failing love,
Drown'd they all thy cares and sadness,
   Sent thee to thy home above.

But I cannot live without thee;
   I am sinking to the tomb;
And, since thou hast gone before me,
   It has lost all shade of gloom.

E'en in fancy now I see thee
   Hovering o'er my dying bed,
With a glittering robe around thee,
   And a wreath upon thy head.

And those speaking eyes are gazing
   On me as in days of old,
And thy gentle hands are raising
   O'er my head a crown of gold.

Oft my arm is raised to clasp thee,
   But it falls through vacant air,

And a chilling wave comes o'er me,—
    'Tis the surging of despair.

I am sinking, I am sinking
    Deep beneath the frozen tide ;
Of its brackish waters drinking :
    Still thou floatest by my side.

Jesus, bear me through the river
    Safely to the other shore,
Where the weary rest for ever,
    And no arm shall part us more.

Now, within the golden city,
    Borne on joyous wings we fly,
Towards His throne whose gracious pity
    Made it life for man to die.

———◆———

THE DEATH OF WOLSEY.

AND Wolsey died amid the quiet monks,
    And lay in state in the old convent hall ;
And many came and gazed upon the corse
Who would have cringed to meet his glance before
And many smiled, as smile the stars, to see
The sun which hides them pass below the west.—
Thus his sun set, though shorn of every beam
That makes the death of day most beautiful.

It melted into mist; the glory went
Before his race was fully run, and left
Nought save the cold, unseemly shape that sheds
Its sombre crimson through the sombre sky,—
A mocking semblance of a glorious past
Drawn earthward by the fog, and darkened by the
blast.

MARY QUEEN OF SCOTS.*

TO thee there stands a monument more fair
　　Than those that, chisell'd by the sculptor's care,
Are spoiled by time, or scathed by ruthless flame;
Their place forgotten—yea, perhaps their name.
Thy crystal shrine increases year by year,
Whose form is moulded by the mountain's tear.

*　　　*　　　*　　　*

O'er Leven's wave the moonbeams sparkled bright,
Touching the placid lake with trembling light,
Whilst the dim shadows that her waters cross'd
Seem'd like dark ebony with gold emboss'd;
And, as grim spectres clad in misty grey,
Four rocky islands on her bosom lay.
There, where the waters kiss the pebbly strand,
The lofty turrets of a fortress stand;

* The introduction refers to a stalactite in a Derbyshire cavern,
bearing Mary's name.

And, hard beneath this castle's frowning wall,
Where darkest o'er the lake its shadows fall,
Was moored a bark, half resting on the shore,—
The ardent Douglas holding light the oar;
Whilst in the stern a figure fair was seen—
The queenlike form of Scotland's crownless queen.
A maiden thrust the fragile bark from land,
Then turned the postern keys with trembling hand,
And in fear's tremour flung them from the bank :
They met the lake, and 'neath dark ripples sank.
Now the light skiff has left the friendly shade,
And o'er the lake a silvery pathway made,
Whilst longer grew the curling foam-flakes hoar,
As the strong rower neared the southern shore.
Soft o'er the waters, like a distant knell,
Floated the music of the convent bell,
And from its Gothic chapel, sparkling bright,
Through every window streamed the fitful light
Of blazing torch, and waxen tapers fair,
In ruddy beams athwart the midnight air.

'Twas through such scenes that fortune sped to shore
The fairest queen that Scotland ever bore :
Her graceful form, her golden tresses light,
Her youthful mien, and eyes so softly bright,
All spoke like plaintive music to the ear,
" Blush for my faults, but grant my fall a tear."

MISCELLANEOUS.

MISCELLANEOUS.

"HE STOOD BETWEEN THE LIVING AND THE DEAD."

THE earth is shaken;—darkness spreads the
    sky,
Save where the lightning whirls its lurid brand,
And shows their pallid cheeks who fear to die
'Neath the dark vengeance of Jehovah's hand.
Whole troops of slain lie prostrate on the sand;
Death plies his sickle with a murderous power;
Plague breathes his noisome fevers thro' the land;
And drought withholds the ever-welcome shower,
Whilst Israel's armies droop, as droops a fallen flower.

The thunder rolls 'mid Sinai's riven stone;
The red-bolts shatter on its barren height,
And all the heavens seem to start and groan,
And the blue lightnings quiver at the sight.
For lo! the glory of Jehovah's might—
Borne on the winds, and wrapt in awful fire—

Dims the round sun, and pales its golden light
In the dread grandeur of His awful ire,
And threatens instant death and desolation dire.

But Aaron stands,—calm, fearless, and alone,
With flowing robe, and priestly mitred head ;—
He mediates with Him upon the throne ;
He stands betwext the living and the dead.
Still is the air,—no distant warrior's tread
Breaks on the awful silence of the camp ;—
No light is there, save the dim, lurid red
That fitful shines, as shines the midnight lamp,
Flickered by gusts of wind, and mists, and vapours
    damp.

In hideous heaps, with ghastly faces, lie
Those who have perished by the noisome blast ;
Their glazéd vision turned towards the sky,
Where, to the great tribunal, spirits passed ;
Then o'er the sky a pale, wan light is cast,
And the clouds break with many a contrary wind ;
These in great heaps towards the west are massed,
And the veiled sun in glory beams behind.
The plague is stayed ;—the clouds with silvery light are
    lined.

THE WIDOW OF NAIN.

THE daughters of Nain are in sackcloth to-day,
    And mourning they stand round the motionless
        clay
Of a youth who has parted from trouble and strife,
From a mother's fond kiss, and the springtide of life.

Like the moan of the rapids, when Jordan is high,
Was heard in the evening that pitiful cry ;
Like the snows of the mountain, when sunlight is fled,
Was the pallid and motionless face of the dead.

And there was the widow, who mourned by the side
Of the prop of her age, and the son of her pride ;
And sad was her visage, and bowed was her head,
Her eyelids were swollen, and feeble her tread.

But the bearers have halted,—the bier is laid down
'Mid the hopes of the poor,—neath the Pharisee's
        frown ;
For the might of Jehovah is shown in the land,
And the fetters of death are unloosed by His hand.

Like the sunbeam that trembles and breaks through the
        storm,
So the first flush of life tinges faintly his form,
That a moment before had seemed dark in the gloom
Of the death-mist that rose from the mouth of the tomb.

The mother was happy, and the people were glad,
And the teardrop was dried from the face of the sad;
As the rainbow that glitters when sunlight appears,
So bright was the blending of soft smiles and tears.

'Twas thus that the Christ of redemption and love
Worked wonders below, and brought life from above,
Plucked the brand from the burning, the dead from the
  grave,—
For the Son of Jehovah is mighty to save.

NAPOLEON III.

BRIGHT shone the Star of Destiny from high,
 And in its ray a lordly city grew
'Neath the all-watchful presence of his eye
Who dazzled millions, but made friends of few;
And used his sceptre with that subtle art
That quells the fire, but ne'er can win the heart.

Then a wild blast came sweeping from the north;
Before it rolled the fierce red tide of war;
And Teuton legions in a wave burst forth,
And drove the Empire, stranded, on the shore;—
Then a cloud came, and, 'midst a cold regret,
The glorious Star of Destiny was set.

THE FALL OF METZ.

THE pride of France has fallen : mourn her fate !
   Mourn for the country blindly desolate,
That, like the transient blossom of a day,
Blooms in the morn, at evening fades away,
And feels the strong and hardy northern power
Coil slowly round her each succeeding hour.
And must her sons lie murmuring in the dust ?
The sword is broken—yet it need not rust.
Must civil combat weaken every vein,
And from her body all her vigour drain ?
Tears are for women, not for men, to shed
O'er cities lost, and comrades stark and dead.
Unite, or perish ! raise your drooping eyes,
Or bow to Fortune's rod, and, yielding, rise !

SHALL THE SWORD DEVOUR FOR EVER?

UNHAPPY France ! o'er thy fair field shall fall
   The blight of conquest and the weight of thrall ;
Gaunt Famine too, with slow and lingering pain
Shall wither those the war-flames have not slain ;
And Pestilence shall rear her ghastly head,
Tainting the air with sightless heaps of dead.

Sad, blighted country ! where is now thy star
That scattered beams of glory wide and far ?
The northern blast, so chilly and so high,
Has torn thy favourite planet from the sky !
Thy vineyards blighted, and thy sons oppress'd,
Oh say, fair country, where is now thy rest ?

Combined and conquering Germany ! thy sway
May rule the hour—ne'er can last the day.
Though all the earth be wrapped in crystal snow,
The deadly, unseen snake yet lives below ;
When spring-time comes, it rears its spotted head,
And pays its annual sacrifice of dead.
Woe to the man, rejoicing in his power,
Who treads where subtle eyes in shadow lower !
Though the small fangs but lacerate the heel,
More deadly is the thrust than hammered steel ;
Through every vein the burning venom flies,
And death is written in the glazing eyes.
Thus though the foe of France ride o'er the plain,
In the long grass her head will rise again,
And ceaseless carnage, and eternal feud,
Shall stain the rivers with whole nations' blood.

December, 1870.

A WAIF FROM THE DELUGE.

SHUDDERING on Ararat he stood,
    And saw the waters wild,
And sadly looked upon the flood,
    And sadly on his child ;
And the infant clapped his hands and smiled,
      And the waters swept beneath.

Close at his feet, his wife lay low,—
    Her cheek was pale and cold ;
And the ripples kissed her feet of snow,
    And played with her ringlets gold ;
And it seemed as if the waters bold
      Paused ere they bore her away.

And the father cried in sorrow,—
    The infant's smile was gay,
For it knew not that the morrow
    Would bear its life away,
Nor that dark cold ripples in their play
      Had numbed the form he loved.

Far o'er the waters' heaving breast
    The ark rode on the wave,
And it seemed in calm and peaceful rest
    To float o'er Nature's grave,—
A refuge powerless now to save,
      Its door fast closed by God.

He stretched his hand towards the ark,
  And cried with agony ;
And lo ! afar, he saw a spark
  Come floating buoyantly,
And he strained his longing eyes to see
    Till they scarce could see at all.

It grew into an angel bright,
  Who caught away the child,
And bore it on his pinions light ;
  And the father sank and smiled,—
For now amidst the waters wild
    He could calmly meet with death.

———◆———

THE ANGEL'S TEAR.

I SAW an Angel wing her joyous flight
  Through all the starry fields of heaven's light,
Till, like a meteor wrapped in silvered snow,
Glittering she darted to the earth below ;
Then passed through tracks of bleak and desert land,
But left no footprint on the yielding sand.

    *   *   *   *

Weary and faint, without a breath of air
To cool the scorching rays of sunlight's glare,
Worn Haroun lay, whilst fierce delirium's pain
With fancies maddened all the fevered brain.

As music calls the charméd snake to die,
False views of plenty met his restless eye,
Then passed from sight in the vast desert air,
And woke the keener frenzy of despair.
Then came the Angel in her glittering dress,
And looked on Haroun in his sore distress;
And as she passed, there fell a crystal tear
That sprang into a stream of water clear;
And near it grew a strange and stately palm,
With mellow fruit his wondering eye to calm.
The Arab quenched his thirst and ate again,
And, like the drooping arum after rain,
Rose vigorous from his desolate distress,
And roamed once more the boundless wilderness;
But ere he parted, turned towards the mere,
And named it " Fountain of the Angel's Tear."

EVENING BELLS.

HOW sweetly do the bells of even
　　Ring out athwart the dewy air !
Like some stray melody from heaven,
　　That scatters gladness everywhere.

In measured tones, and deep vibration,
　　They fill the valleys all around,
And seem to blend the whole creation
　　In tranquil harmony of sound.

Oft when I wander, sadly thinking
　　Of those now far away from me,
They rouse my weary spirit sinking,
　　And make my heavy steps more free.

• Then looking back, the sky is azure ;
　　But looking round me, all is drear ;
And looking forward, through the vapour,
　　Soft gleams of sunshine still appear.

And then the bells, with music teeming,
　　Invite me to the house of prayer ;
Their pensive sadness sets me dreaming
　　That those who are not still are there.

And when the music strains are ringing,
　　I seem to hear their voices clear
In graceful harmony still singing
　　From fancy-painted forms of air.

But e'en when lingering at the portal
　　Till all the varied throng pass by,
Those fading forms I deemed were mortal
　　Dissolve in ether, and I sigh.

———◆———

ODE TO A STAR.

O HAPPY Star, that rests on the bar,
　　The bar of the Milky Way,
Or cradled sleeps where the young moon creeps,
　　When night has o'ermastered the day ! '

From hour to hour each folded flower
  Is pearled by thy tears as they fall
In dewdrops bright, through the cloudless night,
  And glisten on hamlet and hall.

When, breaking forth, the lights of the north
  With glory fill the sky,
Through their rosy veil, serene and pale,
  Shines the calm light of thine eye.

When all below is wrapped in snow,
  And the icicle ferns o'er the pane,
Thou peep'st from thy shroud of drifting cloud,
  And gladdenest the traveller again.

When the ocean lies, like the glass of the skies,
  Unruffled by tempest or wave,
Thy silver hue, enamelled in blue,
  Reflects o'er the seaman's grave.

When pestilence stalks in the crowded walks
  Of the sullied haunts of men,
Like an angel fair, distilling the air,
  Thou breathest forth freshness again.

When earth is no more, my spirit shall soar,
  Shall soar to the homes of the blest;
At thy crystal gate I will joyfully wait,
  And enter on endless rest.

Now morning is gay, and thy fitful ray
  Must pale in the paling blue ;
And the dwellers on earth must wait for thy birth
  Till the fall of the evening dew.

———◆———

THE FUNERAL OF THE BRIDE.

HUSH ! the passing bell is tolling,—
  Hangs a moment on the breeze,—
Then, like distant thunder rolling,
  Sounds through all the churchyard trees.

All the air seems steeped in nectar,
  Gay and bright is every form ;
Tolls the bell like some grey spectre,
  Herald of the coming storm.

See ! grim death among us glancing,
  Grimly stalking by our side,
Round the sparkling wine-cup dancing,
  Tears the blossoms from the bride.

Yonder crowd are gaily twirling
  To the music's merry sound ;
Death, a moment 'mid them whirling,
  Drags the fairest underground.

See ! the long procession winding
   Slowly through the churchyard gate ;
Scalding tears are almost blinding
   The mourning and the desolate.

" Earth to earth "—to earth returning ;
   " Dust to dust "—where dust is spread ;
" Ashes "—no life's flame is burning,
   Till God's trump shall wake the dead.

FAREWELL TO A FRIEND.

FAREWELL ! sweet friend of a fleeting year !
   Sunshine be thine, though clouds be here !
Swift be thy journey ! sweetly fly thy hours,
Garnished with love, and strewed with many flowers !
Though dark my way, of thy sweet light bereft,
I see the rainbow that thy path has left,—
A link to bind this cold and sterner land
With thy far distant, lovely, southern strand,
Where borne by fancy o'er its airy line,
I visit daily at thy beauty's shrine.

THE BITTER ENDING.

I.

MY cheeks are pale, my eye is dim,
    My hair grows grey before its years,
Slow palsy shakes through every limb,
I dwell amidst horrors and fears.

For the leaguering creditors come and go,
Threatening, and branding, and cursing me so;
And old friends ride on, as I used to ride,
But they pass me by on the other side.

And ever there sits at the door of my hall
A poor, wasted form in a scant, tattered shawl,
And a miserable child, that cries all day,
Till—wretch that I am—I drive her away,
Though the fault is mine, and mine the shame,—
I have branded her with a harlot's name!

II.

The night is chill, but I will out and see
What brandy and music can do for me.
By heavens! what is here—so chill and white,
Pale, icily pale, in the icy night?—
She's lying in the frosty light of the street,
All frozen, and mute, and dead at my feet;
Her cold hands are spread as though still in prayer;
The icicles cling to her clustering hair;

A childish and innocent smile, long fled,
Returns once again to the voiceless dead,
And her fingers clasp the baby who rests
Unconscious across her pale mother's breasts.

III.

Mine, mine the ill !—that chilly blood
Grows dark around me, like a flood ;—
This dagger doth its part full well,
Sending a devil back to hell.

IV.

It is over ;—leave me now,—
The death-dew clings to my guilty brow,
And the fiends look out from the gathering dark,
And my life dies down like a flame's last spark.
Spirits of evil!—old faces some ;—
Brandy! brandy !—they come ! they come!

SCENES IN DREAMS.

I DREAMT that I had wings to fly
From clime to clime, from sky to sky ;
And that my airy pathway went
Through all the earthly firmament.

One morn, I paused to rest awhile
Upon the fair and lovely isle
That, girded by Tyrrhenian's wave,
And hollowed by a magic cave,
Seems like a child from Eden born
To beautify this earth forlorn,—
A little Paradise of love,—
A wandering sunbeam from above.

Around me spread a sea of glory
Surpassing all that pen can show;
Vesuvius, queen of tragic story,
Was slumbering in her robes of snow,
Whilst all Tyrrhenian's waters rolled
In one vast sea of liquid gold.

But man, where'er his path has trod,
Is enmity 'gainst love and God;
No earthly scene so passing fair
But you may find a devil there.

Thus, where I stood, two brothers came;—
Within their hearts revenge's flame
Had deadened every deeper thought,
Which separates 'tween *can* and *ought*.

Now face to face they sternly stand,
The toy of death in either's hand;
The word is given, and they fall,
Each stricken by the deadly ball,
Whilst o'er their forms is seen to bend
The man miscalled their mutual friend.

The younger lay cold, stark, and dead;
The morning breeze passed o'er his head;
So fair his lips, though void of breath,
They seemed a mockery of death;
His golden locks, all dyed with gore,
Shall be a mother's pride no more;
And on that reckless youthful breast
The wild sea-gull shall build her nest,
And summer heat and winter storm
Shall pass unheeded o'er his form.

The other, when the shock was o'er,
Rose from the pool of human gore,
Gazed wildly on the prostrate dead,
And vainly bathed the lifeless head,
Whilst terror and remorseful pain
With madness filled his reeling brain.
How could he meet the tearful eyes
Or hear the long impassioned sighs
Of her, the harmless sport of fate,
Whom he had rendered desolate?
He could not think;—he could not bear
The cloudless sky and balmy air,
Nor the calm glory of that sun
Which shone upon a murdered one;—
He leapt the rock's steep, rugged side,
And sunk for ever in the tide.

Eternal darkness and unbroken sleep
Closed o'er him, and he perished 'neath the wave;

No friends to mourn him, and no sons to weep,
Nor raise a monument beside his grave !
A little ripple, and the scene is o'er,—
The waters flow on calmly as before.

    *   *   *   *

Wearied with such a scene, I rose,
Nor lighted till I saw the snows
Of that bleak land which sages say
Has but one night and one long day.
All the sky was bathed in light,—
All the stars were chill and pale,—
And the Aurora of the night
Was the herald of the gale ;
From the Zenith's point it went,
Lighting rocks of adamant,
Glistening on eternal snows
With the colours of the rose ;
Paling to a silvery light,
Strange and beautifully bright.

I lingered in that world of snow
Till round the sky a crimson glow
Told that the summer of the north,
In midday splendour would come forth.
Onward, I passed from day to day
By coral isle and rocky bay,
O'er flowers that bloom where men's feet have not trod,
Seen alone by the unseen God ;
O'er many a hamlet that nestles near
The mountain tarn, or level mere ;

By cities glittering with temples of light,
Golden, or granite, or pure marble white ;
By giant peaks that wrapped in cloud
Stand snowy in their snowy shroud.

Then I reached a valley fair to see,
With citron, palm, and lotus tree ;
Upon each side the hills rose high,
With verdure towering to the sky;
The sun was bathing either height
With golden beams of orient light ;
The butterfly commenced its play
Where dells of fragrant blossoms lay ;
The scarlet poppy glowed all bright,
Opening from the sleep of night ;
The balmy breath of morn was bless'd
With odours from the rose's breast.

But carnage waves her spoiling hand
Above the fairest, loveliest land ;
Death wanders through the odorous bowers,
And blights the bloom of the rarest flowers.
To-day two hostile Moorish bands
Will rein their steeds, and draw their brands ;—
To-night, the stray moonbeam will rest
Upon the lifeless warrior's breast,
Whilst yon pure stream, defiled with gore,
Shall line with corses all its shore ;
For Selim's son has stolen aside
Bedredden's young and fairest bride

And he will win her from his power,
Or die in battle's dangerous hour.

Now the arms are clashing loud,—
Whirls the dust in a rolling shroud !
See ! no quarter here is given ;—
"Allah ! Allah !   Death and Heaven !"
Where the dead are lying deep,
There Bedredden's sabres sweep,
Thin the ranks of turbans green,
Spread confusion o'er the scene.
Backward now fast fall the foe,—
On, Bedredden's army go ;
And, ere evening flushed the sky,
Few remain to bleed or die.

The captive bride, set free again,
Hastens through pathways paved with slain,
Whilst lurid, through the sultry night,
The watchfires glow with fitful light.

But there is a murmur in the camp ;
And here and there a midnight lamp
Gleams for a moment in the vale,
Like fireflies in an Eastern tale ;—
Bedredden nowhere can be found,
Nor near the stream, nor on the ground ;—
   No one saw him fall that night,—
   Many saw him bravely fight.

The Bride is wandering here to seek
  The warrior of her early love,
Like an angel's form, still pure and meek,
  Descending from the stars above.

    She roams the field in raiment fair,
    With step as noiseless as the air,—
    And jetty locks whose sombre bloom
    Is rival to the raven's .plume,
    And silken lash that softly lies
    Over her dark and tearful eyes. '

And he lies there in the pale moonlight ;—
His hair is matted, his cheek is white,
And his eyes, that were of yore so bright,
    'Are closed and lifeless now.

She's coming near to his mossy bed ;
The cold stars gaze on his lifeless head,
And around him there lie the silent dead,
    And a shivered brand by his side.

She's coming,—how can she bear to view
The unconscious form of one so true ?
How. will she mark the blood-stained hue
    That rests on his. pallid cheek ?

• She has found him at length ;—her hands are spread
Above his bowed and his bleeding head ;
Her warm tears over his brow are shed,—
    ' But he'll never hear her call.

To the starlit fields of the upper air
Her eyes are raised in the silence of prayer,
As though she could watch the angel's care ;
   That wafts his soul to the sky.

Slowly she sank upon his breast,—
For ever closed her weeping eye ;—
So slowly sank she to her rest,
Without one parting moan or sigh ;
Like a fair angel, softly weeping,
Above the dead her vigils keeping.*

———◆———

METEORS.

YE meteors, that shoot through the channels of
  space,
Streaking with silver the dome of the sky,
Sailing in ebon with eminent grace,
Fading from sight in the glance of an eye,
Spanning the earth in a moment of flight,
Borne on the wings of the star-loving night ;

Oh ! say, are ye flung from the gates of the day,—
Shot by a whirlwind unspeakably far ?

---

* Moore has the following well-known lines :—

 " While that benevolent Peri beamed
  Like their good angel, calmly keeping
  Watch o'er them till their souls shall wake."

Or bear ye a message, enshrined in your ray,
To the dwellers on earth from some sky-buried star?
Clad in your livery of prism-like hue,
Bordered with crimson and woven with blue.

And have ye been born but, like man, to decay,
To shine for a moment, then vanish from sight,
Worn by the breath of thy swiftness away,
Burnt by the fire that glows in thy light,
Dissolving in ether, or buried in earth,
Unknown in thy death and unseen in thy birth?

THE END.